Be Seal Smart with Brian

By Kinessa Knight

May 2025

About the Author

Kinessa Knight was born in Wolverhampton and currently is residing in Derbyshire with plans to relocate to East Yorkshire, is a dedicated writer with a deep-rooted passion for marine life, especially seals. With a background in education as a former tutor, Kinessa is committed to inspiring curiosity and respect for the natural world.

Her writing is driven by a desire to share knowledge, foster understanding of marine mammals and encourage greater environmental awareness.

This book reflects her lifelong fascination with the sea and its incredible creatures.

Dedication

To my late father, Tony Butler, a magician in every sense of the word, whose creativity and talent as a published writer continue to inspire me every day.

And to my mother, Sue, a retired chartered librarian whose love for books and storytelling sparked my passion for literature from the very beginning.

This book is for you both, with all my love and gratitude.

Chapter One: A Fine Day for a Swim

The North Sea was particularly lively this morning. Gulls screeched overhead; the waves slapped playfully against the cliffs of Flamborough Head. Beneath the surface, a very fine-looking seal was gliding through the water with the effortless grace of a creature that had spent his whole life in it. That seal, in case you were wondering, was me --**Brian**.

Now, I know what you are thinking. Brian? Not exactly the name you would expect for a sleek and powerful grey seal, right? Something like Stormbringer or Wave Crusher might be more fitting? Well, let me tell you something I did not choose it. The humans did.

A group of them, standing on the shore with those little clicky boxes they carry. One of them pointed at me and said, "He looks like a Brian." And that was that.

But I digress. Back to my swim.

I flicked my back flippers, propelling myself forward with surprising speed. Most of the time, I keep a leisurely pace, but when I need to like when a juicy fish is darting away, I can hit speeds of up to twenty-five miles per hour. Not bad, eh? The secret is all in the flippers: my back one steers like a rudder, and my front ones act like wings, slicing through the water with precision.

Today's agenda? A little breakfast, a little sunbathing, and a nice nap.

First, breakfast. The North Sea is a giant buffet if you know where to look. Cod, herring, sand eels are delicious. I scanned the water with my big round eyes (excellent for seeing in low light, thank you very much) and caught sight of a silvery flicker. Ah-ha! Herring.

I exhaled a stream of bubbles and dived

deep, twisting, and turning as I chased the slippery little snack. The herring zig-zagged, but I had the advantage. You see, my whiskers' properly called vibrissae are not just for looking handsome. They can detect the tiniest movement in the water, making it nearly impossible for a fish to hide from me. One quick lunge and GULP. Breakfast, sorted.

With a full belly, it was time for a rest. You might be wondering: Brian, how does a seal sleep in the water? Excellent question! We doze off in a few ways. Sometimes, I will float on the surface like a very handsome buoy, bobbing along with the waves. Other times, I will sink down to the seabed and hold my breath while I nap (yes, I can hold my breath for over thirty minutes, but I do not like to brag). And on lazy days, I just rest with half my brain awake because yes, we can do that. It is like sleepwalking, but in the sea.

I surfaced near the cliffs, basking in the golden morning light. A couple of my fellow seals were already lounging on the rocks,

4

looking smug. Sunbathing is essential, it helps us warm up after long swims in the chilly North Sea. Unlike those annoying otters who have super thick fur, we seals rely on a lovely layer of blubber to keep warm. Functional and stylish.

As I flopped onto the rocks, I sighed in contentment. Another perfect morning.

Little did I know, this day was about to get a whole lot more interesting… but that is a story for later.

Right now, it was time for a nap.

Chapter Two: A Proper Nap and a Bit of People Watching

Ah, now this was the life.

I lay sprawled on the golden sand, my plump, blubbery belly warming under the morning sun. Every now and then, a gentle sea breeze ruffled my fur, carrying the salty scent of the waves. My big, round eyes blinked slowly, moist, and glossy just the way they should be. Unlike those land-dwelling creatures, we seals do not have tear ducts, so instead, our eyes stay nice and hydrated with a special mucus. Sounds gross? Maybe. But it keeps them from drying out, which is important when you spend half your life in salty water.

I wriggled my body slightly, getting comfortable, and then, with the grace of a creature that does not care who is watching,

I scratched my side with my back flipper. Ohhh, that is the spot.

Seals may look sleek and smooth, but we shed our fur once a year, and in between, it gets itchy. Scratching is essential. If you ever see one of us flopping about, flicking a flipper to our side or rubbing our heads with our front flippers, we are not just showing off we are getting in a good scratch.

As I lounged, I could hear the chatter of humans in the distance. A few of them were walking along the beach, admiring me from afar as they should. They were keeping a respectful one hundred metres away, which is just how I like it. Any closer, and I would have to give them the look you know, the one that says, "Oi, personal space, please!"

I could tell they were watching, taking those little clicky pictures they love so much. I lifted my head slightly and gave them my best profile. Might as well make sure they got my good side.

Out in the water, a group of kayakers were paddling past, their brightly coloured boats bobbing on the gentle waves. I lifted my head, interested but unbothered. Humans in the sea did not bother me much, they were not fast enough to be a threat, and they were not tasty enough to be food. Still, I kept an eye on them. You never know with humans. Sometimes they did silly things, like trying to get too close to seals in the water. Not today, though these ones were behaving themselves, paddling along and pointing in my direction.

I was about to settle back down when a sound made my whiskers twitch.

A bark.

Not a seal bark oh no, that is a lovely sound. This was a dog bark. And it was getting closer.

I turned my head, and sure enough, a large, excitable looking dog was trotting along the beach, yapping away as if it had important business to deal with. Its human was holding onto a lead, keeping it from getting too close - good human. I have no problem with dogs, but let us be honest, they can be a bit much. They do not understand personal space, they do not know how to relax, and worst of all they sniff everything.

I let out a slow exhale through my nose, unimpressed, and flicked some sand over my back with my flipper. A good seal does not let trivial things ruin his rest.

The sun was rising higher now, warming my fur, making me feel heavier and sleepier. I let my head rest against the cool sand and sighed contentedly. My breathing slowed, my heart rate dropped, seals have this wonderful ability to slow our heartbeats right down when we rest, which helps us conserve energy. We do it even more when we dive deep into the sea, but right now, it was simply for the sake of a nice, relaxing snooze.

I closed my eyes. The humans could watch, the kayakers could paddle, and even the dog could yap. Brian was having a nap. Nothing was going to ruin that.

Well… almost nothing.

Chapter Three: The Invasion of the Tourists

I was having the best nap. The sun was warm, my belly was full, and apart from the occasional yap of an overenthusiastic dog, life was peaceful.

Then, suddenly voices.

"Oh my God, look! A seal!"

"It is so cute! Quick, get a picture!"

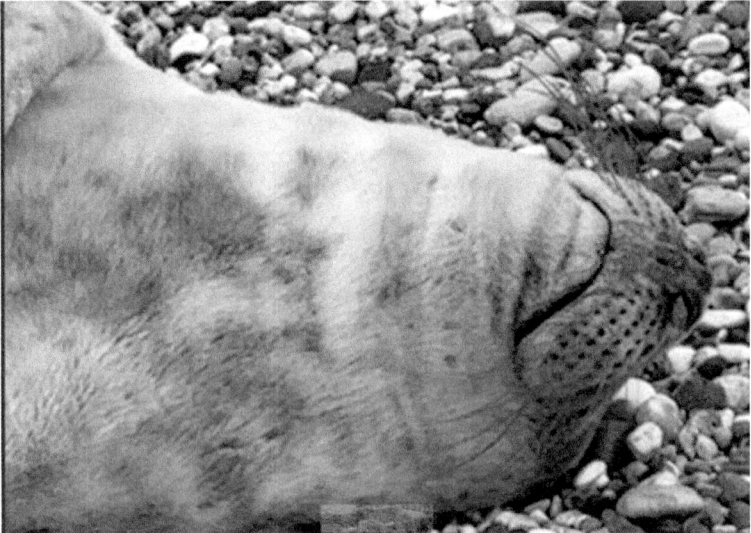

I cracked one eye open. Two humans, one man, one woman was walking straight towards me, holding those little glowing rectangles they always seem so obsessed with. I sighed heavily through my nose. Here we go…

Now, do not get me wrong. I understand that I am incredibly handsome. My smooth grey fur, my big, soulful eyes, my impressive whiskers, what is not to admire? But there is a difference between appreciating me and invading my space. And these two? They were getting far too close.

They were not at the respectful hundred metre distance like the earlier tourists. No, they were creeping forward, muttering to each other. I could feel their eyes scanning me, and I could sense what was coming before they even said it.

"Do you think it's okay?" the woman whispered.

The man frowned, tilting his head. "I dunno… It is not moving much."

I groaned internally. Of course I am not moving much, I am napping! But humans have this strange belief that if an animal is lying still, it must be in trouble.

Newsflash: We like to rest!

I opened both eyes and gave them a clear warning look. They did not take the hint.

"It looks stranded," the man said. "Should we… should we put it back in the water?"

Oh, for blubber's sake.

Now I was annoyed. First, they woke me up. Then, they invaded my space. Now they were talking about shoving me back into the sea as if I did not know how to seal properly?!

I did the only logical thing. I opened my mouth wide, bared my impressive teeth, and let out a deep, guttural growl.

"RRRUUURRRRGHHH!"

The humans jumped back.

"Oh my God, it's angry!" the woman gasped.

"Duh," I thought.

Grey seals like me have a full range of noises. We growl when we are annoyed, bark when we want to warn others, and even make clicking sounds to communicate underwater. This growl was my way of saying, "Back off, human, or I will make this very awkward for both of us."

The couple hesitated, but instead of leaving, they started talking more.

"Maybe it's injured," the woman said, frowning.

"It doesn't look hurt," the man replied, eyeing me. "Maybe it's just sick?"

I sighed so loudly I nearly blew sand into my own face. Why do humans always assume something is wrong when a seal is on land?

We come onto beaches all the time. We rest, we sleep, we digest our food. And no, we do not need to be "rescued" and shoved back into the sea like some kind of lost fish. We are marine mammals, which means we live both in the water and on land. If I wanted to be in the sea, trust me, I would be in the sea.

But the damage was done. The couple's loud voices had attracted more humans.

A small crowd started forming, more people with cameras, pointing and whispering. Some children were squealing in excitement. And then, oh, the horror, one of them shouted:

"IT'S A SEA LION!"

I almost choked on my own indignation.

A sea lion?! A SEA LION?!

I turned my head sharply, fixing the child with my most offended glare. If I could speak human, I would have given them a full-on biology lecture. But since I cannot, let me clear this up right now:

I am a seal. Not a sea lion.

Sea lions have ear flaps. Look at my head, do you see ear flaps? No. I have little ear holes, perfectly streamlined for swimming.

Sea lions have long front flippers that they use to walk on land. Me? My front flippers are shorter, and I must do a very dignified (and slightly wobbly) belly flop to move around.

Sea lions are loud, noisy, and constantly barking. Grey seals like me? We prefer a good growl when annoyed and a deep, mysterious underwater call when we want to be impressive.

In short: I AM NOT A SEA LION.

But did the humans listen? No. They kept talking. Kept pointing. Kept clicking their little picture boxes.

And all I could do was sigh dramatically, flick some sand over my back, and hope that eventually, they would get bored and leave me in peace.

Chapter Four: The Selfie Saga and the Perils of Geotagging

There I was, minding my own business, attempting to resume my much-needed nap after the earlier human hubbub, when I noticed a peculiar phenomenon. The crowd of humans on the beach was not dispersing; in fact, it was growing. More of them arrived, armed with those little glowing rectangles they seem so fond of. I overheard snippets of their chatter:

"Saw the post about the seal, had to come see for myself!"

"It is trending everywhere! #BrianTheBeachSeal"

Ah, social media, the human obsession with sharing every waking moment.

Now, I do not mind a bit of admiration.

After all, I am magnificent. But things took a turn when the phrase "Let's take a selfie!" started circulating among the crowd. Humans began edging closer, angling their devices, attempting to capture themselves with yours truly in the background.

This did not sit well with me. Not only was my personal space being invaded, but I was also starting to feel a tad threatened. So, I did what any self-respecting seal would do: I bared my teeth and let out a deep, guttural growl. It is important to note that while I may look cuddly, I am still a wild animal with a set of sharp teeth. Approaching seals for selfies is not only unwise but can also be dangerous. In fact, conservation groups in the UK have been advocating for laws to prevent such disturbances, as they can cause significant stress to seals and even lead to health issues.

My display of displeasure caused some humans to step back, but instead of leaving, they began discussing among themselves.

"Maybe it's stranded?" one suggested.

"Should we call someone?" another pondered.

Oh, for the love of fish! I am perfectly fine, just trying to enjoy a bit of sun and sand.

Seals often haul out on beaches to rest, digest, and warm up. It is a natural behaviour and does not necessarily indicate distress.

As the day wore on, I noticed another troubling trend. Humans were not only taking photos but also sharing them across various platforms, Instagram, Facebook, TikTok, and even LinkedIn. Each post was accompanied by tags and geotags pinpointing my exact location.

Now, I may be a seal, but even I understand the implications of this digital age behaviour. Geotagging, while it may seem harmless, can lead to an influx of visitors to specific locations. This surge in foot traffic can disturb wildlife habitats, lead to environmental degradation, and increase the risk of harm to both animals and humans. For instance, geotagging has been linked to habitat destruction and wildlife displacement as more people are directed to previously secluded areas.

Moreover, not everyone who sees these posts has good intentions. Broadcasting the exact location of wildlife can attract individuals who may exploit or harm animals. There have been instances where geotagged photos have led poachers directly to endangered species. While I may not be endangered, the principle remains the same: sharing precise locations can pose risks to wildlife.

So, while I appreciate the admiration and understand the excitement, I implore humans to exercise caution. Enjoy the moment, take a mental snapshot, and if you must share, do not put the exact location. It is a small step that can make a significant difference in protecting creatures like me and the environments we call home.

Now, if you will excuse me, I have a nap to return to, hopefully, this time without any further interruptions.

Chapter Five: The People in Orange

Just as I was settling back down, after the whole selfie saga and the great geotagging disaster, a new development caught my eye.

A small group of humans were walking towards me, but these ones looked different. For one, they were not waving their little picture taking devices around. And more importantly, they were wearing bright orange tabards.

Ah. I knew exactly who they were.

The medics.

They are a group of humans who know what they are doing. Unlike the rest of the crowd, who thought I was either a celebrity or a lost puppy, these medics had been trained to handle situations involving seals, whales, and dolphins.

A sensible human must have called them, concerned about me, thinking I was in trouble. I had mixed feelings about this.

On one flipper, I was annoyed. I was not in distress! I was just trying to have a perfectly normal rest on the beach, and now I had a group of high-vis humans walking towards me with a sense of purpose. But on the other flipper, I was relieved. Finally, someone who might explain to the crowd that I did not need rescuing, nor did I require an impromptu photoshoot.

The lead medic, a woman with a calm, reassuring voice, began speaking to the gathering tourists.

"Alright, folks, we appreciate your concern, but this seal is fine. Seals come onto land to rest, and they should be left alone. Please give it space, at least one hundred metres."

Thank you! Finally, someone who gets it!

She continued. "We are here just to check on its health and make sure there are no signs of injury. But please do not approach and do not try to push it back into the sea, seals know where they want to be!"

I shot the earlier "rescue mission" humans a pointed look.

The medics started their assessment. I stayed still but watched them closely. Unlike other humans, who seem to act on impulse, these ones observed first. They checked my breathing (normal), my eyes (bright and clear), and my movement (strong and well fed). They also looked for injuries, none, obviously, because I am a very capable seal.

One of them noted my size and said something that made me rather pleased:

"He is in good condition. Nice blubber layer."

Why, thank you. I have been eating well.

These medics are volunteers trained to respond to marine mammals in trouble. If a seal really was sick or injured, they would know what to do, sometimes monitoring from a distance, other times stepping in to relocate an animal if needed. They even help with stranded whales and dolphins, which, I must say, sounds far more dramatic than dealing with grumpy seals like me.

They are a charity, meaning these humans were not being paid to do this, they were doing it because they care about marine animals. That is quite nice, really. Even though I found them slightly annoying, I had to respect their dedication.

Satisfied that I was healthy, the medics turned back to the humans.

"Alright, let us give him some space. If you want to take photos, do it from a distance. No selfies, no crowding, and no tagging his location online."

Now that made my whiskers twitch with delight. Finally, someone telling these humans what I had been trying to say all day!

With a final glance in my direction, the medics stepped back, making sure the crowd also moved away. I exhaled slowly, allowing myself to relax again.

These orange tabard humans were not so bad after all.

Chapter Six: My Very Own Bodyguard

Ahhh, finally. The crowd was thinning.

One by one, the humans lost interest. They had taken their pictures, posted their #SealDrama updates, and once they realised, I was not going to juggle fish or perform a backflip they shuffled off to buy ice creams or stare at the sea like they had never seen it before.

Honestly, good riddance.

But not everyone left.

One of the medics remained, standing a respectful distance away. I glanced at her out of the corner of my eye. She was not taking selfies. She was not talking at me. She was just… watching.

Ah. My own personal bodyguard.

I approved of this. Having someone sensible around meant that tourists would (hopefully) think twice before doing anything particularly foolish like trying to poke me with a selfie stick or, worse, pet me. (Seriously, humans, I am not a Labrador.)

She had a walkie talkie clipped to her belt, a handbook in her pocket, and most importantly an air of authority. She also had a no-nonsense attitude when it came to dogs.

"Excuse me," she called to a passing tourist whose large Labrador was trotting towards me, ears perked up with far too much enthusiasm. "Can you put your dog on a lead, please? There is a resting seal here."

"Oh, but he's friendly!" the owner chirped, beaming like this was helpful information.

The medic did not budge. "I am sure he is, but seals are not. He could get scared, and if he feels threatened, he will defend himself."

I flicked my flipper in approval. Exactly. I had very sharp teeth, and I would use them if necessary. Not because I am mean, but because no seal wants a giant wet nose shoved in their face while they are trying to nap.

The tourist grumbled but clipped the lead onto the dog's collar and walked on. Victory.

As my new bodyguard stood watch, a few stragglers wandered up and started asking her questions. Some were sensible. Some… not so much.

Sensible Tourist: "How long do seals usually stay on the beach?"
Medic: "It depends! Some just rest for an hour or two, others might stay all day. They haul out to digest their food, warm up, or simply take a break from swimming."

(I nodded approvingly. Absolutely true.)

Mildly Confused Tourist: "Is it lost?"

Medic: "Nope! Seals are meant to be on land. This is perfectly normal."

(THANK YOU! I nearly clapped my flippers in appreciation.)

Wildly Incorrect Tourist: "Can it breathe out of water?"

Medic: Blinking in disbelief "Yes. It is a mammal. It has lungs, just like you."

(I gave the tourist a look. Honestly, humans.)

Excitable Child: "Will it do tricks if we give it fish?"

Medic: "Absolutely not. This is not a performing seal. It is a wild animal, feeding it would do more harm than good."

(Exactly. I am not a circus act, and besides, the fish humans eat is different from the fresh, nutritious seafood I catch myself.)

Elderly Tourist: "I once saw a seal balance a

ball on its nose on TV. Can they all do that?"

Medic: "Nope! That is something sea lions are trained to do in captivity. Wild seals do not do tricks for entertainment."

(I sighed dramatically. Sea lions. Again.)

The questions kept coming. Some were good, some were questionable, and some made me question how humans manage to function in the wild at all.

But at least my bodyguard was handling it all well. She stayed firm but friendly, making sure everyone understood that I was fine and that the best thing they could do was leave me in peace.

Eventually, the last of the stragglers wandered off, and the beach became quiet again. Just me, my bodyguard, and the sound of the waves.

I gave a deep, satisfied sigh and stretched out in the sand. Peace at last.

For now.

Chapter Seven: Back to the Big Blue

I had done my time on the beach.

I had napped. I had digested my fishy feast. I had tolerated tourists, survived selfies, and even acquired my own personal bodyguard. But now, the sea was calling me back.

It was time to return to my true home the vast, rolling waves of the North Sea.

With a deep sigh, I stretched my flippers, gave my whiskers a good shake, and prepared for my grand departure. Of course, as with all things in life, getting onto a beach is far more graceful than getting off one.

Seals do not have the long, powerful front flippers that sea lions use to walk across land. No, we move with a more… dignified technique called the seal shuffle, a combination of bellyflopping and wiggling that is both highly effective and incredibly awkward looking.

So, in a series of elegant (read: clumsy) scoots, I began my journey back to the water.

The sand beneath me grew cooler and wetter as I approached the shoreline. The waves rushed forward to meet me, swirling around my flippers, welcoming me back like an old friend. The saltwater tingled against my skin, washing away the sand and the stress of the day.

But just before I fully submerged, I turned back.

My medic bodyguard was still standing there, watching me go.

For the first time since she arrived, she was not answering questions, moving people along, or keeping overexcited dogs at bay. She was just watching, a small smile on her face.

I do not speak human, and she does not speak seal. But for a moment, we understood each other perfectly.

Thank you for looking out for me, I thought.

And with that, I pushed forward, slipping into the water with ease.

The second I was fully submerged, I felt alive again. My body, built for this world of weightlessness, moved effortlessly through the currents. I twisted, turned, and dived, revelling in the freedom of the sea.

Beneath the surface, the world was a different place. The sounds of the beach faded away, replaced by the soft, distant clicks of fish, the occasional song of another seal, and the steady, rhythmic crashing of the waves above.

I swam deeper, twisting my body in a way I never could on land, and released a few contented bubbles from my nose.

I was home.

And as I disappeared into the endless blue, I could not help but think that, for all their flaws, some humans were not so bad after all.

Final Chapter: Brian's Message to the World

Alright, humans this is Brian, the seal, and I have got something important to say. After all the adventures I have had on the beach, the crowds, the selfies, the medics, and the whole lot of excitement, I want to share something important with you all. It is time for a little chat about seals, and how we all can get along in this big, beautiful world we share.

So, here is the deal: We seals, like me, are wild creatures. We are not pets, we are not zoo animals, and we do not like being treated like part of the local tourist attraction. We are part of the wonderful natural world, and it is essential that we get the space and respect we need to live our lives in peace. If you ever find yourself near a seal, here is what you should and should not do:

What to Do:

1. Keep your distance – If you see a seal, stay at least one hundred metres away. This is roughly the length of a football field, so it is plenty of space to admire us from a safe distance. We are wild animals, and when we are resting on the shore, we need our personal space.

2. Enjoy us from afar – If you want to take photos, great! We look pretty adorable, I know. But use a zoom lens and stay back. No need to get up close. If you are too close, it can make us stressed, and we might run back into the water before we are ready.

3. Respect our need for rest – We seals need time to nap and recuperate. Think of us like your friendly neighbourhood cat, lounging around in the sun. Do not rush us. If we are napping, we need that time to rest up for more adventures, like swimming and hunting.

4. Keep your dogs on leads – We are not fans of excited dogs rushing around us. It can make us nervous, and they might chase

us into the water, which is not ideal. So, if you are walking your dog near us, please keep them on a lead to make sure we are all safe and happy.

5. If you spot a sick or stranded seal, contact a medic – If you see a seal that is injured or stranded on the beach, please contact a medic or a local marine rescue group. They will know exactly what to do and will make sure I or any other seal gets the care we need.

What Not to Do

1. Do not approach us – I know, I know. We are cute, and I have that rugged seal look, but please, do not come too close. Approaching us can cause us stress, and we might end up leaving the beach prematurely, which could make us tired and not in the mood to go back out for food or fun.

2. Do not feed us – I know it is tempting, but do not feed us. While it might seem like a nice gesture, it can mess with our natural hunting habits. We know how to find our

own food, feeding us can lead to health problems. Plus, you would not want me following you around looking for snacks all the time, would you? Let us keep the boundaries, please.

3. Do not take too many selfies – Seriously, no one needs to see me from that close. Taking pictures is fine, but a group of tourists crowding around me for selfies? Not cool. I am not a model; I am just trying to relax and do my seal thing. Let us keep it respectful!

4. Do not leave rubbish behind – This one should go without saying, but it is always important to make sure the beach stays clean. We seals can get entangled in rubbish, and it can be dangerous for us. Be sure to take your rubbish with you, or better yet, pick up a piece of litter if you see it.

So, there you have it. A little bit of respect and a little bit of space is all we ask for. And it is not just about me, Brian the seal. It is about making sure all of us, the seals, the birds, the sea creatures, and even the seabirds, have the chance to thrive in our home, the wild ocean.

If you treat the sea and its creatures with respect, I promise you will have an unforgettable experience. You will be able to see us in our natural habitat, doing what we do best swimming, playing, resting, and just enjoying the ocean like we have done for generations. It is a magical thing to witness, and we want to share it with you, as long as it is done in the right way.

So next time you see a seal, remember this: Give us space, respect our needs, and let us be wild. You can admire us from a distance, and who knows? Maybe one day, you will be lucky enough to spot a new pup, or maybe even share a moment with a seal like me.

But whatever happens, remember that we seals, whether common or grey, young, or old are part of this beautiful, wild world. Let us keep it that way, together.

With that, I am off to catch some fish. Until next time, my friends! Stay wild, stay respectful, and keep the sea magical.

The end. Or is it?

My dear friend Alice has her story.

Be Seal Smart with Brian

By Kinessa Knight

Through Alice's eyes

By Kinessa Knight

Chapter One: Through Alice's Eyes

The world has always been a beautiful place for me, though sometimes it is hard to see through my tired, salt encrusted eyes. I am Alice, and I have lived most of my long life on the East Coast of Yorkshire.

I was born on the cliffs of Flamborough, where the sea crashes against the rocks and the salty wind sings through the heather. I have swum in these waters since I was a pup, and they have known me well. My body has become one with the waves, and the tides know my name. But time, as it does for all things, has passed, and now I am no longer the young, curious seal I once was.

I am an elderly lady, as you might say,

though I prefer to think of myself as wise. At the grand age of twenty-four, I have seen much, and the sea has taken me to many places. The waters around Flamborough, my home, are full of life, those cliffs and the great colony of seals that gather here. You can see us from the shore if you are patient and respectful, resting in the sun or slipping beneath the waves to hunt for fish. We are part of the landscape here, always present, always moving with the seasons.

As a young seal, I ventured far from Flamborough once or twice, swam down the coast, and even further, across the bay, to see what the world beyond my birthplace was like. Seals do swim far; it is in our nature. We follow the currents, feel the pull of the open ocean, and let our instincts guide us to unfamiliar places. But no matter how far I swam, there was always a pull that called me back, back to the cliffs and the rocky shores of Flamborough. Perhaps it was the familiar scent of the seaweed, or the way the waves crash against the rocks, always loud, always constant. Perhaps it was the colony, my family, scattered across the rocks and beaches, as dependable as the tides. I have never been one to stay away for long.

I have birthed many pups in my life, sixteen, to be exact. The first few were hard, as they always are, but I learned quickly, as we all do. The ocean is a hard teacher, but one who only wants the best for you. Each time I brought a pup into the world, I would stay close, resting on the beach with them for weeks, keeping them safe and warm. I would teach them the ways of the sea, the soft ripples of the water, the rush of the waves, and how to find the fish that feed us. For a seal of my age, I have seen many generations come and go. Some pups, like my own, grow up strong and healthy. Others, though, drift away, lost to the harshness of the world. But the ones who make it… they return to Flamborough, just as I do. It is where we all belong.

The colony at Flamborough has always been a refuge for us. It is a safe place, where we can rest on the rocks after a long swim, where the young pups learn to swim before they venture out into the vastness of the sea. It is a place where the sea feels like home, where it understands us, and we understand it. But this place, like all places, is changing. I have seen it. The tourists come now humans, standing on the cliffs with their strange, loud voices and those curious little devices in their hands. They do not understand us, not really. They do not know how to give us the space we need.

But the ones who do, the ones who stand back and give us our space, they are the ones who see us for what we truly are magnificent, magical creatures, worthy of respect and awe. The medics are one of those who understand. They know to keep their distance. They know the guidelines at least one hundred metres away from a resting seal. If I feel threatened, I will move away, but if they are too close, I will make it known. I will growl and show my teeth, a warning. It is not just to keep myself safe; it is to keep my pups safe. Stress can cause us to abandon our pups, or worse, leave them vulnerable to predators. The medics know how to help us when we need it, and they are careful not to disturb us when we rest. I have seen them before, rushing to help a young seal or a struggling pup, doing what they can to ensure the safety of our kind.

I am old now, and I do not swim as far as I once did. The currents tire me more, and the long journeys take their toll. But I am content. Flamborough is home, and it will always be. I have seen the pups grow, seen them learn to dive beneath the waves, and it fills my heart with joy. One day, my pups will have pups of their own, and they will come to the same place I did, just as I always return.

For now, I rest. The sun is warm on my back, and the sea calls to me, gently, as if it knows my time is near. But even though I am old, there is a peace in knowing that the sea will always be there, that Flamborough will always be home. I close my eyes for a moment, allowing the waves to rock me gently, and I smile, a seal's smile, perhaps a quiet, happy thought that I have lived a good life, in the place where I belong.

It is a good life, and the sea, like me, will go on, always.

Chapter Two: A Young Seal's Struggle

When I was just a pup, everything was new. The world was so big, and the ocean seemed endless. The soft ripples of the water, the gentle pull of the current, and the warmth of the sun on my back as I rested on the rocks of Flamborough, all of it was so exciting, so full of promise. But as I grew older, I learned that the sea, like all things, could be both beautiful and dangerous.

I remember one day, when I was young, just a few months old, really, venturing farther from the colony than I ever had before. The tide was high, and I swam near the shoreline of Bridlington, not far from the cliffs I called home. The sea was full of life that day. Fish darted past, and the waves were playful. But then, something caught on my neck, something sharp and unfamiliar. I did not know what it was at first, just that it made me feel trapped.

It was a fishing net, tangled around my neck like a strangling band. I thrashed about in the water, panicking as it tightened, its fibres cutting into my skin. The more I struggled, the worse it got. The weight of it pulled me down, and I fought to keep my head above water. It was not the first time I had heard of seals getting caught in nets, many of my friends had been through it, but in that moment, I did not fully understand how serious it was. I was just a pup, and my instincts were all I had.

The pain was sharp. The net scraped my skin, and I could feel the weight of it dragging me down. My heart raced; my breaths shallow. I tried to swim free, but the more I fought, the tighter it seemed to pull. I started to lose strength. I was scared, scared of what might happen to me, of what the net might do if it did not come off.

I was not alone for long, though. As I struggled, I heard voices, human voices. It was strange to me then; humans had never been so close. They were a part of the world

I had only heard stories about. But they were here, and they saw what had happened.

It was a woman in an orange tabard, one of the medics. She moved quickly and calmly, the way I had seen the others act when they came to help. There was something in the way she approached me, with such care and quiet understanding, which made me trust her, even as I fought the fear that gripped me.

She was quick, using her hands to gently untangle the net from my neck, speaking softly as she worked. I could hear her voice, though I could not understand the words. It did not matter. The touch of her hands was soothing. With every movement, she pulled the fibres free, the sharp sting of the net easing as it loosened. I could feel my breath returning to normal, the panic fading away. Soon, the net was off. The fecling of relief was like a wave washing over me. I could breathe again. I could swim again.

But the sea, while beautiful, was not always kind. The medic could see that I was not fully recovered. There were small wounds on my neck, where the net had cut into my skin, and I was weak from the struggle. She knew what needed to be done. Rehabilitation was the next step.

They took me to a safe place, far from the dangers of the sea for a while, where I could rest and heal. The rehab centre, full of other seals who had been hurt or sick, was quieter than the colony, but it was warm and safe. The humans who worked there, like the medic who had rescued me, took care of us. They gave me medication to help my wounds heal, and they fed me, letting me regain my strength.

I remember the tubs of fish they gave me, so fresh and delicious, that I almost forgot about the pain. The water was warm there, and the other seals would come and go. Some were still too young to understand what had happened to them, but I knew. I had learned a valuable lesson: the sea, for all its wonder, could be a dangerous place, especially when humans did not respect it or when the fishing gear, they left behind became deadly to us.

Some of my friends had been caught in nets too caught in the same way I was. It happens far too often, especially when humans leave fishing nets behind, or even when they do not dispose of them properly. Ghost nets, as they call them, are one of the biggest threats we face. They are abandoned nets that drift in the water, waiting to entangle anything that gets too close. It is not just seals that suffer from them, but dolphins, turtles, and birds too.

I remember, in rehab, hearing the stories of others who had been entangled. There was an old seal, who had been caught as a pup, and another who had nearly drowned before a kind human had found her. It was always the same humans coming to the rescue, pulling us from danger when we could no longer help ourselves. They do not always know what it means to us, but I do. I know they save lives, and I will never forget what they did for me.

But after the wounds healed, and I was

strong again, I was ready to go back. Ready to dive back into the sea where I truly belonged. The rehab centre gave me the chance to recover, but the sea, it calls to me in a way nothing else does. It was my home then, and it is still my home now.

Now, every time I swim, I am a little more careful, a little more aware. I am older now, and I know the dangers of the sea. But I also know the beauty of it, and the joy of swimming free, of feeling the waves beneath me and the wind in my fur.

And I never forget that the medics, those amazing people in their orange tabards, are there, always watching, always ready to help when we need them.

Chapter Three: Kevin – My First Pup

Ah, Kevin. My first born. What a little troublemaker he was and still is, I imagine. Thinking back to the time I was carrying him, I cannot help but smile, despite all the changes it brought. The pregnancy, for a seal like me, was not quite like what the humans might experience. For starters, there is no morning sickness or cravings for odd things like pickles. Instead, we seals go through a slow, steady change, and we feel it in every part of our bodies. It is like the sea itself is rearranging you, preparing you for something much bigger than you can imagine.

Pregnancy for a grey seal lasts about eleven months, which is longer than most mammals, but not long enough to get used to the idea. You feel it from the inside out, the slow expansion of your belly, the weight on your back, the way the tides feel different. During this time, you cannot swim as fast as usual, not because you want to be lazy, but because your body just does not work the same. It is like trying to swim with a big rock tied to you. It is a bit of a challenge, but you just get on with it, because there is a little one growing inside you, and that little one is the most important thing in the world.

During my pregnancy, I could not do a lot of the things I normally enjoyed. For instance, my favourite diving spot, the one where the fish gather in the deepest part of the bay? Well, I had to leave that one behind. Not because it was not nice, it was, but it was too deep and too much effort to get to. And let us not forget the constant need for rest. I mean, we seals are known for resting, but during pregnancy. Oh boy, it is like being extra lazy on purpose. I would find a nice spot on the rocks and just flop there, basking in the sun, occasionally giving my belly a little pat.

Sometimes, I would think to myself, is this what it is like to be a human? So much time spent lounging, feeling the world gently rock beneath me. I did not have the energy for long swims, though I would take short dips in the shallows when the sun was not too hot.

Then, after what felt like an eternity (but really, it was about eleven months), I finally felt it, the stirrings of my pup, Kevin. My body knew what to do. It was a strange sensation, like I could feel him wiggling, making his presence known in the most subtle of ways. The big day came, though, when I felt that unmistakable shift. Kevin was on his way, and I had to get ready.

The birth was quick, much quicker than I expected. It was not painful, like I had imagined. It was more like a slow, natural unfolding, a wave that comes gently and does not crash. Before I knew it, there he was, a tiny bundle of fluff and wet fur. The first thing I noticed was how tiny he was. Not much more than a few kilograms (I think, I did not really weigh him with a scale, obviously!). I could not help but stare at him, his big, dark eyes staring back at me with that innocent curiosity all pups have.

At first, Kevin was a bit clumsy, like most pups. He would wriggle and try to stand on his little flippers, then topple over like a sack of fish. He was always hungry, of course, what pup is not? But that meant I had to keep close watch on him, nursing him and keeping him warm. I remember how small he felt next to me, like he could slip right between my flippers if I were not careful.

It is funny, but during that time, I never really thought about myself. All I could think about was keeping Kevin safe and making sure he learned how to swim. I would nudge him into the water, showing him how to float and kick his little flippers. At first, he did not get it, he kept sinking like a stone, but I stayed patient. Eventually, he figured it out, though it was not pretty. His little flippers were more like the sails of a boat in a storm, flapping wildly until he finally steadied himself.

Seals do not keep their pups for long. I stayed with Kevin for about three weeks, just long enough for him to learn the basics and get strong enough to swim on his own. After that, I had to let him go. I know, it sounds cold, but that is just the way we are.

It is how we have survived for so long. We teach our pups to be strong, to survive on their own in the ocean, where the currents are unpredictable, and the world is always changing.

Some people think that is sad, but for me, it is the natural way. I did not want Kevin to depend on me forever, so I let him go, trusting that he would grow into a strong, independent seal, just as I did.

Did I still see him after that? Well, that is the funny part. Seals are not like humans. We do not have those long-lasting connections, the way you might with family. We are more solitary, more independent by nature. But sometimes, when I am out swimming, I will see Kevin from a distance. He is grown now, as seals do, swimming with the rest of the colony. Every now and then, I will catch a glimpse of his dark eyes, and I wonder if he remembers me. Maybe he does, but the sea has a way of making us forget certain things, things we do not need to survive.

But as I swim through the waters of Flamborough, I like to think that, in some small way, I will always be there for him, just as I was when he was a pup. After all, that is the bond we share, even if we do not always see it.

And when I see him swimming with the others, I cannot help but think, well, I did an excellent job. I gave him the tools he needed to thrive out here, just as my mother did for me. In the grand scheme of things, which is what really matters.

Chapter Four: Love, or Something Like It

Now, let us get one thing straight, seals do not do romance. There are no long walks on the beach, no candlelit dinners, no whispered sweet nothings under the moonlight. When it comes to love, we grey seals keep it simple: meet, mate, move on.

That is how it was with Dwight, Kevin's father. Oh, Dwight. What a beast of a seal. He was a bull seal, one of the big guys, easily weighing in at 300 kg (six hundred and sixty pounds), probably more, if you counted the sheer amount of blubber he carried around. He was not exactly what you would call handsome, unless you have a thing for battle scars, a scarred-up nose, and a smell that could knock a seagull out of the sky. But he was strong, and in the world of seals, that is what matters.

I remember the first time I saw him that year, during the breeding season. The bulls arrive first, hauling themselves onto the beaches of Flamborough, ready to fight for their place. And when I say fight, I mean it. Seal bulls do not just politely ask to be in charge, they bellow, lunge, and bite their way to the top. Dwight was no exception.

He had a booming voice, one of those deep, guttural "HARRRR-HARRRR-HOOOORH" sounds that echoed across the cliffs, warning other males to stay back. And if they did not? Well, let us just say, I saw Dwight send more than one challenger rolling back into the sea, bruised, and beaten. The fights were brutal, open-mouthed clashes, biting, shoving, and the occasional body slam. The strongest bulls win the best spots on the beach, and the best spots mean the most females.

So, there I was, one of many females on the beach that season, waiting for the chaos to die down. The air smelled of salt and seaweed, mixed with the distinctive musky scent of the bulls. And once the battles were over, the real business began. Dwight was victorious, standing tall (well, as tall as a seal can stand) among the others. He had earned his right to be there, and we females took notice.

Now, do not get me wrong, I was
not choosing him. That is not really how it
works. Seals do not form lifelong pairs like
some animals do. We do not settle down and
raise our pups together, sharing parenting
duties. No, it is all about survival of the
fittest. Dwight had proved he was strong,
and that was enough for me.

The actual mating part? Well, I will not get
into the details, it was not exactly romantic.
It was quick, it was business, and then…
that was it. He moved on, as bulls do,
looking for his next conquest, and I went
back to the sea, carrying the future
troublemaker that would become Kevin.

Did I ever see Dwight again? Oh, plenty of
times. He showed up every breeding season,
a little bigger, a little more scarred. Bull
seals can live up to twenty-five years, and
they do not slow down until they must. Each
year, he had come roaring back to
Flamborough, challenging younger bulls,
still fighting for his spot. I even spotted him
once while I was out swimming, just a

massive shadow gliding under the waves, his wide head breaking the surface now and then. We did not acknowledge each other. There was no "Oh hey, remember me? The mother of your pup?" That is just not how it works in the world of seals.

I do not know where Dwight is now. Maybe he is still out there, still fighting, still chasing after the next female who happens to be on his beach. Or maybe he is finally lost a battle and given up his spot to a younger, stronger bull. That is the way of things. The ocean is a tough place, and even the biggest, strongest bulls do not stay on top forever.

But one thing is for sure, he left his mark, literally and figuratively. Kevin, my firstborn, was proof of that.

Chapter Five: Little Victoria

Victoria. My beautiful little pup.

She came into this world on a crisp, cold morning, her fur still wet from birth, her tiny flippers trembling against the chill. She was perfect, as perfect as a grey seal pup could be. She had the softest white lanugo coat, like fresh snow, and big, dark eyes that seemed too wise for a newborn. I knew from the moment I saw her that she was special. She was strong, lifting her little head almost immediately, searching for me, her mother. And she was clever, wriggling closer to my side, instinctively knowing where warmth and comfort were.

She weighed, maybe 15kg (thirty-three pounds)? A solid little thing, round and plump, just the way a newborn should be. As I nuzzled her, breathing in her scent, a mix of salt and something new and precious, I felt something I had not known before. A different kind of love. A love that made me want to protect her from everything in the world.

I did everything I was supposed to do. I fed

her my rich, fatty milk, thick and nourishing, just as my mother had fed me. With each feeding, she grew stronger. Her cries were loud, demanding, so full of life. I rested beside her on the beach, watching over her as the waves lapped at the shore, my body shielding her from the wind.

But the sea is not always kind.

It had been a rough season. The tides were higher than usual, the storms came more often, and the wind howled through Flamborough's cliffs like a warning we could not understand. The beach was crowded, too many seals, too many bodies pressing close together for warmth and space. It should have been safe. It should have been enough.

But then, one night, the storm came.

I remember the rain hitting hard, each drop cold as ice. The wind screamed through the darkness, and the waves grew angry, crashing higher up the shore than they ever should. I tried to keep her close, curling around her, shielding her tiny body with mine. I knew she was scared; I could feel her little heart racing, her small flippers pressing against me for warmth.

Then, when the tide surged, it happened. A massive wave rolled in, higher, stronger than anything I had ever seen. It rushed through the beach, sweeping pups from their mothers, tumbling them into the cold, merciless sea.

I fought. I fought so hard.

I thrashed and called for her, my voice lost in the storm. I searched in the dark, my heart pounding, but she was gone. Just gone.

Pups are born on land because they cannot swim at first, their fluffy white coats are not waterproof. If they are taken too soon by the sea, they do not stand a chance. I knew that. And yet, I kept searching. I searched until the storm faded, until the sun rose weakly over the horizon, casting its pale light over the wreckage the sea had left behind.

And then I saw her.

She had been carried too far, her tiny body lying still on the wet sand. My beautiful, strong, clever Victoria was gone.

I nudged her, willing her to wake up. But there was no breath, no movement, no life. The thing I had loved so fiercely, the little being I had fought to protect, was lost to the ocean.

This is the way of the sea.

Some pups do not make it. Many do not survive their first few weeks, lost to storms, predators, or simply the harshness of the world into which we are born. It is a truth I have known my whole life but knowing it does not make it hurt any less.

I stayed with her for a long time. The other seals had already begun moving on, life in the colony never stops. But I stayed. I let the waves lap at my flippers, let the wind dry the tears I did not even know I had. And when the tide rose again, I let the sea take her back.

I do not know where she rests now. Maybe she has become part of the waves, part of the current that moves through this vast, endless ocean. Maybe she is simply gone. But I remember her. I will always remember her.

And the next time I gave birth, when I nuzzled my new pup close, I whispered her name into the wind.

"Victoria."

Chapter Six: "Wait… SEALS DO WHAT?!"

Now, I consider myself a seal of great wisdom. I have lived through storms, dodged sharks, and survived motherhood (which, let me tell you, is harder than dodging sharks). But nothing, nothing, prepares me for the absolute nonsense that comes out of humans' mouths when they see us.

I spend a lot of time lounging on beaches, and let me tell you, if seals had a hobby, mine would be eavesdropping on humans. It is hilarious. You would not believe the things I have heard people say about us.

The "Seal" ions Debate

One of my favourites is the classic: "Mummy, look! A SEA LION!"

Oh dear. No.

Let me clear this up for the last time: we are
not sea lions. They live in warmer places,
have big ear flaps, and can walk on their
flippers like some kind of acrobatic weirdo.
We, on the other hand, slither. We do
not walk; we shuffle like a sleepy human in
slippers. If you ever see a seal "walking"
toward you, congratulations! You are in
California or dreaming. Wake up.

"Is it Dead?"

Now, I love a good nap. We seals spend up to 80% of our lives resting (yes, 80%, I have done the math). But humans do not seem to understand the fine art of relaxation.

I once heard a woman scream, "IT'S DEAD! CALL SOMEONE!" after looking at me for about four seconds. Ma'am. I am literally blinking. Do dead things blink? I do not think so.

To be fair, I get it. When we sleep on the beach, we can look a bit… well… lifeless. We do not move much. We drape ourselves across the sand in various dramatic poses, sometimes I like the sprawled out like a melting marshmallow position, and sometimes I go for the face down in the sand I have given up look. Either way, I am fine. I promise.

"Why Don't They Drink Water?"

Ah, a human classic. I heard a man say once, very confidently:
"Seals do not drink water. They just absorb it through their skin like a sponge."

Sir. With all due respect… WHAT?!

We are not walking cucumbers. Of course, we drink water! But here is a cool fact: most of our hydration comes from the food we eat. Fish are basically little swimming water bottles for us. (So next time someone tells you to drink more water, just eat a fish and say you are doing it seal style.)

The UFO Conspiracy.

This one really made my whiskers twitch.

Two humans stood near me once, looking out to sea, and one of them whispered:
"I heard seals are actually ALIENS."

ALIENS.

Because apparently our big eyes and smooth heads make us look like extraterrestrials. First of all, rude. Second, we have been on Earth longer than humans. Maybe they are the aliens, ever think of that?

"That's a shark!"

A personal favourite:

"Oh my god, look at that shark!"

I heard a kid shout this once while pointing directly at me. Now, I am a lot of things, a mother, a survivor, a professional fish enthusiast, but I am not a shark. I do not even have the teeth for it! What shark has a face this cute?

The "Seal Whisperers"

Finally, we have the brave souls who think they can talk to us.

I once watched a man kneel down, look me right in the eye, and say, in a serious tone:

"I know you understand me. Blink twice if you can hear me."

I did blink twice. But that is just because I have eyelids, mate.

Humans are funny creatures. They mean well (most of the time), but wow, they really do believe some nonsense about us. If you ever see a seal, and you are about to say something, just pause. Ask yourself: Would a seal laugh at me for saying this? If the answer is yes… just admire us from a safe distance and enjoy the magic.

Trust me. We are worth it.

Chapter Seven: The Art of Eating (A lot)

If there is one thing I take seriously, it is food. Some seals might say that raising pups is the most important part of life. Others might say it is survival. But let me be honest, what is life without a full belly?

I am a grey seal of the East Yorkshire coast, and I have spent my entire life perfecting the art of eating. The North Sea is my pantry, and I know every single shelf.

What is on the Menu?

People always assume I just eat fish, and they are mostly right. But let me be specific, shall we? I do not just eat fish; I eat the best fish.

• Cod – A solid, reliable choice. A bit flaky, but who isn't after a long winter?

• Herring – Tasty and full of fat, which is great for keeping me warm in winter. I love a good, oily fish.

• Whiting – Not as rich as herring, but easy to catch. I call it a "lazy lunch."

• Flatfish (like sole and plaice) – Tricky little things because they hide under the sand, but oh, the satisfaction when you grab one!

• Sand eels – They wriggle like mad, but I do love a crunchy snack.

How Much Do I Eat?

A lot. A whole lot.

On a normal day, I eat about 5kg (eleven pounds) of fish. But in the colder months, when I need extra blubber, I will push that up to 7kg or more. That is like a human eating fifty cheeseburgers in one sitting.

I do not mess around.

The Catching Game

Catching fish is not as easy as it looks. Some humans think we just open our mouths and fish swim in. If only! No, I must work for my dinner.

I am an ambush hunter. That means I do not chase fish for miles like a crazy dolphin. I wait, I lurk, I hide in the kelp or glide silently under a shoal of fish. And when the time is right, WHOOSH! I snap my jaws shut faster than a human grabbing the last biscuit off a plate.

I can also dive over one hundred metres deep if I need to, and I can hold my breath for up to thirty minutes. That means I can sit there, lurking in the dark like an underwater ghost, until dinner practically swims into my mouth.

The Digestive Situation

Now, let us talk digestion. It is fast.

I do not chew. Chewing is for amateurs. I swallow my food whole or in big chunks. My stomach is like a furnace, it dissolves bones, scales, everything. That is why you will not find tiny seal toothbrushes for sale; we do not need them.

But I do burp. A lot. No one ever talks about that, do they? A full seal is a burpy seal.

Food Fights and Scarcity

Ah, but here's where things get complicated. Not every seal meal is peaceful.

Sometimes, there's just not enough fish to go around. The North Sea has been changing. Humans take a lot of the fish, and I have noticed that winters feel harder than they used to.

And when food is short? Oh, we fight.

You have never seen drama until you have watched two bull seals fighting over a particularly nice herring. They roar, they bite, they slap each other with their flippers. I prefer to stay out of it, I am a lady of grace and dignity, but if someone tries to take my cod, I will absolutely let them know about it.

Stealing is a Way of Life

And here is another secret: we steal from each other all the time.

If I catch a fish and I am too slow to swallow it, another seal might just snatch it right out of my mouth. No apology, no shame. Just gone. Rude.

I once had a beautiful, fat whiting stolen by a juvenile who swam off giggling. (Yes, we can giggle. It sounds like a weird snort.)

I suppose I was just as bad when I was young.

So, there you have it, the great art of eating, seal style. It is not just about survival. It is about knowing when to hunt, where to hunt, and how to keep your fish away from thieving little brats.

Now, if you will excuse me, I saw a particularly nice herring swim by…

Final Chapter: Alice's Wisdom of the Waves

Ah, life. Many long, salty, spectacular years in the sea. That is how long I have been here, longer than most seals, longer than some of the cliffs I rest upon, or at least that is how it feels. I have seen the tides rise and fall, watched the moon pull the ocean in and push it back out again, felt the warmth of summer sun on my fur and the bite of winter storms against my whiskers.

And now, as I float in the great, endless blue, I think about what I have learned.

Lesson One: The Sea Always Wins

You cannot fight the sea. Many have tried, seals, fish, even humans with their strange floating boxes, but in the end, the sea is bigger, stronger, and older than us all. It does not listen to our wishes, nor does it care for our plans.

But if you learn to move with it, to read the waves, to trust in the tides, then you will always find your way home.

Lesson Two: Eat the Fish While You Can

Life is short. One day, you are a sleek young seal diving after herring with the speed of a torpedo. The next, you are a wise old lady who moves a little slower, lets the younger seals go first, and savours every fish she catches.

So do not hesitate. Take the fish. Enjoy the moment. Because you never know when the tide will turn.

Lesson Three: Rest is Just as Important as Swimming

Some creatures are always moving, always rushing, always looking for something just beyond the horizon. But seals, we know better. We know when to swim, and we know when to stop.

I have spent whole afternoons basking on the sand, my flippers warmed by the sun, my eyes half closed as the world drifts by. And do you know what? Not once have I regretted it.

Lesson Four: Humans are… Odd, But Mostly Kind

Oh, the things I have seen. Tourists mistaking me for a shark. Children screaming "IT'S A SEALION!" at the top of their lungs. (I am not but thank you for your enthusiasm.)

But I have also seen the gentle hands of medics cutting me free from fishing nets. I have seen humans stand guard as I rested on a busy beach, making sure no dog or curious child got too close.

Yes, there are fools among them. The ones who take selfies too near, or try to feed us their sandwiches (please, no more ham and cheese, I eat fish, thank you). But most of them? Most of them care. And that gives me hope.

Lesson Five: Love Comes in Many Forms

I have loved deeply in my lifetime. My pups, even the ones I lost. The bull seals I have shared seasons with, even though none of them ever remembered my name.

I have loved the sea, even when it was cruel. I have loved the land, even when it was crowded. And I have loved the quiet moments, the silver moonlight on the waves, the gentle hum of the tide rocking me to sleep, the sound of gulls calling to one another in the morning.

Lesson Six: We Are Not So Different, You and I

You, reading this. You are not a seal (unless you are, in which case, hello, dear). But we are not so different.

We all need space. We all need respect. We all need time to rest and time to swim.

And, most importantly, we all belong to this world, the cliffs, the beaches, the sea itself. So, take care of it. Take care of us.

I am Alice, daughter of the waves, mother of many, survivor of storms. I have lived, I have loved, I have laughed. And when the tide finally calls me home, I will go knowing that my world, our world, is full of life, full of beauty, and full of stories yet to be told.

Swim wisely, my friend. And never forget to enjoy the fish.

Through Alice's eyes

By Kinessa Knight

A thank you from Kinessa Knight

From windswept cliffs at Flamborough
Head,
Where sea meets sky and gulls are fed,
A heartfelt thanks I send your way,
For reading my seal tale today.

You have turned the pages, smiled with
care,
At flippers waving in salty air.
Each seal you met, both bold and shy,
Lives near the tides where puffins fly.

So, thank you, friend, for buying my book,
For giving these sea stars a second look.
For learning how to watch with grace,
From sandy shore or clifftop place.

Admire from afar, stay kind and still,
Let nature thrive by wave and hill.
The East Coast calls with every tide,

And now, you are part of that seal side pride.

More tales will come, both near and wide,
With seal-y secrets and oceanic pride.
So, keep an eye on every wave,
For stories of the bold and brave.

With grateful heart and ink in flight,

Thank you again,

Kinessa Knight

If You See a Marine Mammal or Seabird in Trouble

Marine Mammals (Seals, Dolphins, Whales, Porpoises):

If you spot a seal, dolphin, whale, or porpoise that looks injured, sick, or in danger, please contact a trained rescue team. Do not approach, touch, or try to move the animal, they can be easily stressed or may bite.

British Divers Marine Life Rescue (BDMLR)

01825 765546 (24-hour hotline)
www.bdmlr.org.uk
Rescues injured or stranded seals, dolphins, whales, and porpoises around the UK.

RSPCA (Royal Society for the Prevention of Cruelty to Animals)

0300 1234 999 (24-hour line)

www.rspca.org.uk
Responds to injured marine mammals and
seabirds in England and Wales.

SSPCA (Scottish SPCA)
03000 999 999
www.scottishspca.org
For any wildlife emergencies in Scotland.

For Injured or Oiled Seabirds:
You can contact RSPCA (0300 1234 999) or
reach out to a local wildlife rescue centre
near the coast.

Be Seal Smart with Brian
By Kinessa Knight

Kinessa Knight - Author

Follow me on Facebook for more books coming soon.

Search for Kinessa Knight

https://www.facebook.com/share/12JR6mU bZEk/?mibextid=wwXIfr

ISBN: 9798316776610

Imprint: Independently published

Printed in Dunstable, United Kingdom